Miss Nelson Gets a Telephone Call

Written & Illustrated by
Harry Allard

The Lewis Carroll Press
Oaxaca, Oaxaca, Mexico

*I dedicate this book to
James Edward Marshall
who was born in San Antonio,
Texas on 10 October 1942 and
who died in New York City
on 13 October 1992.*

H. A.

SUMMARY

Late one Friday the 13th in November, Miss Nelson gets an alarming anonymous telephone call. She then takes an ill-starred short cut through the dilapidated and soon-to-be-razed Old East Wing. There she stumbles upon something that almost unhinges her mind and that causes her to swoon.

But luckily for her, exactly one week later, and at the very same hour and in the very same spot, an old friend of hers surfaces who, putting her shoulder to the wheel, quickly unmasks the malevolent telephone caller who is bound and determined to oust Miss Nelson from Room 207, nudging her into early retirement, and —with luck— sending her packing to a hospital, clinic, or cozy nursing home specializing in nerve cases.

The plot foiled, both Miss Nelson and her tenebrous alter ego, Miss Swamp, turn up trumps again and carry the day.

It all began late one Friday the 13th in November.

As she did almost every Friday afternoon, Miss Nelson had stayed after school to correct papers and to prepare her lesson plans for the following week.

When she looked up from her desk, it was already dark outside. How early night falls at this time of year, she thought to herself ruefully.

Her work done, she got up from her desk. She put on her coat. She tied a paisley scarf under her chin. She put on a pair of warm, fur-lined gloves.

She switched off the desk lamp. She turned off the overhead light. Then she quietly closed the door to Room 207 behind her.

It was already a quarter past seven and on a Friday night to boot. Except for Old Pops, the ancient senior school janitor, and his two young assistants, there would be very few people still afoot in the Horace B. Smedley School—or so Miss Nelson thought…

As Miss Nelson was passing by the Principal's Office on the first floor, she heard the clicking and the clattering of a typewriter.

The racket was coming from the Principal's Office.

The door to Mr. Blandsworth's office was open, so she looked in.

Ms. April Cunningsgore, Mr. Blandsworth's gabby and not a little dizzy secretary was pounding away at a vintage Remington typewriter as if the Fate of the World depended upon it.

"Still hard at work, April?" said Miss Nelson.

"Yes," April sighed. "Just after lunch Mr. Blandsworth gave me a forty-page, top-priority report to type up in triplicate. He must have it by no later than eight-fifteen this evening, he said."

"What's the report about?" asked Miss Nelson.

"It's about the Price of Tea in China," April said. "The poor man just stepped out for a fresh-baked Danish and a cup of hot java. He certainly could use a pick-me-up. Why he has been wearing himself to a frazzle of late, what with running this big school by day then staying up half the night working on his latest invention. You do know that Mr. Blandsworth is an inventor, don't you?"

"Yes," said Miss Nelson, smiling. "I remember that last year he invented an underwater pencil sharpener called the Aqua-Sharp and the year before that rubber taps for tap-dancers who cannot stand the sound of taps."

Just then the telephone rang.

"It's for you, Miss Nelson," April said. "You can take it in Mr. Blandsworth's private office."

Miss Nelson stepped into Mr. Blandsworth's Inner Sanctum, half closing the door behind her.

"Hello," said Miss Nelson. "This is Miss Nelson speaking. How may I help you?"

At first there was no reply, only the sound of heavy breathing.

Then a muffled voice said, "I've got your number, Miss Nelson, and I fully intend to upset your apple cart—so BEWARE!" Then whoever it was who was calling rang off—Click!

"Hello? Hello!!" said Miss Nelson.

When she emerged from Mr. Blandsworth's office, she was as white as a sheet.

"Anything wrong, Miss Nelson?" said April, looking up from her typing.

"No, April, nothing. Just a crank call."

But Miss Nelson was visibly upset—and frightened too.

Then on top of everything else, she remembered that she had left her car keys back in Room 207.

She said good night to April and ran up the stairs to fetch them.

Her car keys retrieved, Miss Nelson, as she so often did, especially on a Friday evening, took a short cut to the Teachers' Parking Lot by cutting

through the second floor of the moldering Old East Wing. Although it was strictly forbidden, it would save her many steps. And, she thought to herself, who would ever know?

The Graustarkian Old East Wing,
which was built in 1847, was far gone
in decay and smelt of rot and mildew
and of mouse and rat droppings.

A squeaking bat, flapping its leathery wings,
grazed her head. A cobweb brushed against her
cheek. An owl hooted. A dog barked.

Miss Nelson trod the rubble-strewn second-floor
corridor gingerly, lest she stumble and fall.

Then she saw *IT*.

A wan and wavering, sickly yellowish light was filtering out from one of the ramshackle and long-disused classrooms; and, —oddly enough,—the classroom had the very same number as her own classroom: Room 207!

Curious, she peeked through the door window.

And what she saw made her hair stand on end and her blood run cold!

All of her kids were sitting quietly at their desks, but dressed as they would have been dressed over a hundred years ago.

A mysterious woman, who was also dressed as she would have been dressed over a hundred years ago, was sitting quietly at the teacher's desk in front of the classroom; but, owing to the dim light, Miss Nelson could not see her face.

But when the mysterious woman got up from her desk
and stood in front of the blackboard, Miss Nelson, thun-
derstruck, saw that the mysterious woman…

…was she herself, MISS NELSON!

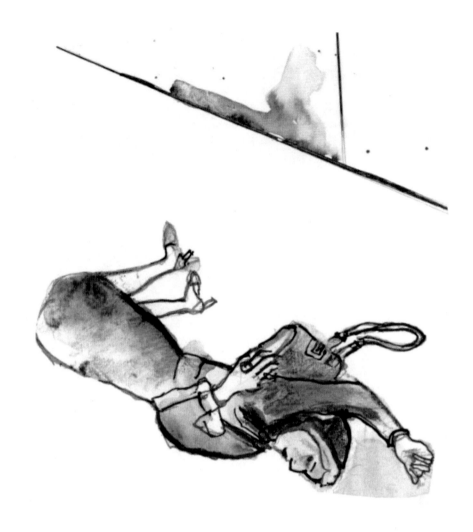

Miss Nelson fainted.

By chance, about a half an hour later Old Pops and his two young assistants were also taking a short cut through the Old East Wing, where they stumbled upon Miss Nelson's body.

They were shocked and appalled.

When Miss Nelson opened her eyes again, the light in the eerie classroom had been extinguished.

"Are you all right, Miss Nelson?" said Old Pops in a quaking voice.

"Shall I call a doctor, Miss Nelson?" said Rudy Jones, who was visibly shaken.

"May I get you a glass of water and an aspirin, Miss Nelson?" said Kevin Jones, who was ashen and aghast.

"No, thank you," said Miss Nelson. "I'll be all right. Really."

But old Pops and his two young assistants were not convinced and they insisted upon accompanying her to the Teachers' Parking Lot.

The three of them resolved then and there to keep an eye peeled and an ear cocked looking out for Miss Nelson's safety and well-being.

The fog and the mist were as thick as split pea soup as Miss Nelson drove home that night.

The bleak weather mirrored her black mood. "There is mischief abroad in the Old East Wing," she said to herself. "And I fully intend to get to the bottom of it, even if I have to call on an old friend of mine to lend me a helping hand."

Exactly one week later, at the same time and in the same place, a bizarre female figure of unknowable age, wearing a battered *Three Musketeers* hat, an ugly dress, and two-tone witchy shoes with arch- supporters, was skirting the peeling and crumbling wall of the second floor of the Old East Wing.

She passed by the empty classrooms one by one —201, 203, 205— until she reached Room 207. As the previous week, a wan and sickly yellowish light was filtering out from Room 207.

She pussyfooted to the warped door and with her claw like, liver-spotted hand grasped the rusty doorknob, took a deep breath, and then, emitting a blood-curdling eldritch shriek, burst into the ghostly gaslit classroom like an Avenging Fury.

A fracas ensued.

The Swamp led with a haymaker and fol-
lowed it up with one or two expertly and
elegantly executed *katas*. [1]

The blond woman standing in front of the
black-board fell to the floor in a heap.

And lo! —unwigged, unmasked, and
uncorseted,—lay…

[1] Please see note at the end of the text.

. . . Mr. Blandsworth, who was alter-
nately bellowing and blubbering.

It was as plain as a pikestaff that he
was as mad as a hatter.

One moment he thought that he was
Miss Nelson, the next, Napoleon.

Scattered all over the classroom lay the dummies that he had fashioned to drive Miss Nelson out of her room and her mind in a fiendish and demented scheme that he had baptized **OPERATION BLACK WIDOW SPIDER.**

Insanely jealous of Miss Nelson's growing national and international fame as a superb grammar-school teacher and as a virtuosic classroom disciplinarian, Mr. Blandsworth had plotted to drive her into permanent early retirement.

But his diabolical plan had backfired; and he —poor, deluded soul, —was hoist with his own petard.

One moment he was yelling, "Unhand me, villains! Don't you know that I was voted Best Teacher of the Year three years ago?"; and the next, shouting, "Avaunt, groundlings! I am Napoleon and I escaped from the Island of Elba in 1815!"

In all the pother, din, and commotion, no one had noticed that Miss Swamp had vanished as if into thin air.

Everyone was surprised and baffled.

Everyone, that is, except for Old Pops, who knew something that no one else knew or could possibly ever know.[2]

[2] Please see note at the end of the text.

Then, to top everything else, everyone's eyes began to smart and everyone began to sneeze.

Someone yelled, "Fire!"

And it was true. The Old East Wing was in flames. And little wonder too. For the Old East wing was as dry as mummy dust; besides which, someone had been monkeying with the ancient gas main of late.

Everyone fled from the burning building.

The Old East Wing burned to the ground before
the firemen could arrive.

Mr. Blandsworth was eventually committed to a lovely private lunatic asylum called Whispering Glades.

His padded cell was beautifully appointed.

On his good days, he cuts out paper dolls; on his bad days—well, why go into it?

He is still convinced that he is Miss Nelson.

Miss Nelson sends him all her old clothes and old shoes. And for Christmas she never fails to send him a homemade fruitcake chock-full of nuts.

The Horace B. Smedley School now has a new Principal.

Her name is Miss Ilona K. Chatterton. The teachers, staff, and kids all love her.

She is firm, but she is fair. And lots of fun too. Sometimes she even plays softball with the 7th and 8th grade boys and volleyball with the girls.

The girls are agog about her stylish clothes.

And talk about efficiency! Why on her very first day on the job she seemed to know the Horace B. Smedley School like her own pocket, from the empty, airless attic down to the Stygian sub-sub-basement.

It was almost as if she had been the Principal of the Horace B. Smedley School in a past life.

Ilona K. Chatterton,
PRINCIPAL

33

The only dissenting voice was that of Eunice P. Scraggs, an old hag who had worked as a cafeteria lady at the Horace B. Smedley School since the Year One.

"There is something fishy about the new Principal," Eunice was never tired of saying, "And that slight foreign accent! What is it exactly—Hungarian, Rumanian, Bulgarian, or Russian?"

And then Eunice would add darkly, "My great-great-grandmother also worked in the school cafeteria
way back when Hector was a pup and she used to tell me about a lady Principal here at the Horace B. Smedley School who also spoke with a slight foreign, eastern-European accent…"

"What was the principal's name, Eunice?" the other cafeteria ladies would ask, half-mockingly.

"I don't remember," Eunice would reply. "My memory is shot. All I remember is that the lady Principal with the slight east-European accent came to a terrible end…"

Thursday is Sloppy Joe Day at the Horace B. Smedley

Eunice was not the only person plagued by doubts about the new Principal.

Miss Nelson also felt that there was something suspicious —and even downright sinister— about Miss Chatterton.

Furthermore, she could not shake off the nagging feeling that she had seen Miss Chatterton somewhere else.

But where, where, WHERE?...

The End

ENDNOTES

[1] Miss Swamp, who was a Black Belt in karate many times over, had spent the past fifteen-odd summers in Outer Mongolia studying under the famous but little-known martial arts master, Ming Chop-Suey.

Here is a rare photograph of Ming. Besides the martial arts, Ming was a bird-fancier—or what is known as an ornithologist.

We see him here pursuing, and about to net, the rare far-eastern wren-sized bird, the titty-boing-boing (unfortunately now close to extinction).

This unusual bird flies backwards and barks like a dog. The female of the species will only nest in the tea cup of the Emperor of China. The yoke of her eggs, when cracked open, yields either a small ruby or a large emerald. When domesticated, the titty-boing-boing can, with love and patience, be taught to dance the Irish jig.

2 A long, long time ago, when Old Pops was still a very young man just starting out on his career as a grammar-school janitor, a very old black woman named Mrs. Beaumont used to drop by the Horace B. Smedley School almost every weekday afternoon to sell her to-die-for homemade glazed doughnuts. Now despite the fact that Mrs. Beaumont—whose given name was Sarsaparilla—looked like a Haitian witch on a bad day, she was highly intelligent, utterly charming, and a sparkling conversationalist withal. Mrs. Beaumont told the then-young Old Pops the following story. And she knew what she was talking about too, for her own grandmother had been born a slave on an okra plantation in South Carolina.

"Originally," said Mrs. Beaumont, "dee Old East Wing had not been a wing at all, but, rather, dee main and only school building. Before dee Civil War, it had served as a way-station on dee Under-ground Railroad by which runaway slaves from dee South were spirited to freedom in dee North.

"Dat is why, Honey-Chil'," said Mrs. Beaumont, rolling her big eyes and lowering her voice to a barely audible whisper, "dee Old East Wing is honey-combed wid secret passageways where, since 1865, only dee unblinking spider spins her tireless web and dee sullen adder lays her baleful eggs…"

The then-young Old Pops gulped and nearly choked on his cherry-flavored glazed doughnut.

Mrs. Beaumont put her stubby right index finger to her lips and whispered conspiratorially, "Mum's dee word!"

Then, brightening up again, she said, "More coffee, Hiram?" —which was Old Pops' given name. Do please take another glazed doughnut. Dees one's on me. I'm especially proud of dee mocha-flavored ones sprinkled wid fresh-grated coconut."

For all queries, comments, and suggestions,
please send your email to:

harrygallard@gmail.com

Coming soon:

Miss Nelson is Scared

12/5/14

Made in the USA
Las Vegas, NV
14 April 2024

88674882R00031